INJURED COUGAR

Love is not all: It is not meat nor drink
Nor slumber nor a roof against the rain;
Nor yet a floating spar for men who sink
And rise and sink and rise and sink again;
Love cannot fill the thickened lung with breath,
Nor clean the blood, nor set the fractured bone;
Yet many a man is making friends with death
Even as I speak, for lack of love alone
It well may be that in a difficult hour,
Pinned down by pain and moaning for release,
Or nagged by want past resolution's power,
I might be driven to sell your love for peace,
Or trade the memory of this night for food
It well may be. I do not think I would.

—*Edna St. Vincent Millay (1892–1950)*

Printed and bound in the United States of America.

ISBN 978-0-98348293-2
Library of Congress registration # Txul-249-992

Book Design and Project Management: Dan Forrest-Bank, FB Edit–Design

Published by
Old Ann Press
P.O. Box 1954
Estes Park, CO 80517
www.oldannpress.com

INJURED COUGAR

A Romantic Fantasy

VIOLET LEE HUNT

OLD ANN
PRESS

To Mary, Joyce and Fran,
my wonderful traveling companions.

Contents

Prologue

A S I LIE HERE in my hospital bed in a drug-induced state from numerous painkillers, my total right knee replacement surgery now over, I begin writing down the early drafts of a romantic fantasy. When I can't sleep at night, I dream about my orthopedic surgeon, 50-year-old Dr. Bradley Hess, whom I find mysteriously attractive.

Each night I add a little bit to my story, writing everything down on a pad of paper. I'm not even sure I can write in my drug-induced state. I don't know if I can capture the unusual stirrings, visions and sensations I have experienced during my three-day hospital stay.

I needed a title for my story to provide an anchor to wrap the story around and to help focus my thoughts, which zip through my brain lightning fast from one hemisphere to the other. My thoughts are centered on three topics: how I feel when fully awake, how I feel when drifting off to sleep or waking up and how all of this relates to the wild cougars that keep appearing in my dreams.

The dictionary defines the word cougar as a middle-aged woman who seeks out younger men for romance or physical intimacy. It also defines the word as an attractive older woman who finds herself in a romantic relationship with a younger man.

Fifteen years ago when I had my total right hip replacement at the relatively young age of 52, I also had a crush on my 40-year-old Boulder orthopedic surgeon, Dr. Harry Render. Something in my psyche is strongly attracted to men of skill who help me. At that time I was on morphine and heard the rehab nurse say that Dr. Render thought I was attractive. That spun my uninhibited creative mind into motion, and I envisioned many scenarios being with him ballroom dancing, hips moving effortlessly together, doing a slow waltz, locked in his arms, wearing a sapphire green velvet cocktail dress and rhinestone necklace.

I could have written a story then using the first new definition for cougar. I don't think such definitions for the word "cougar" even existed twenty years ago. I found it compelling how these definitions relate to people being patterned after predatory animals. When I thought about Dr. Render and I dancing, I envisioned him as a sleek, muscular, narrow-wasted black panther, his strong hands and soft paws moving gracefully over the floor, occasionally pausing and then quietly moving with me again in one effortless motion.

> *Native Americans thought the black panther was a symbol of the dark of the moon and could help people overcome their primitive fears of the dark and of death. The male black panther is a wonderful mix of beauty and purpose. He moves gracefully and can start and stop in an instant. He can freeze in one position for a long time and then quickly move away, hardly making a sound.*

But those passionate imaginings for Dr. Render soon passed. I was too busy trying to get back to work to support my family and home to be thinking about writing a romantic fantasy. As my hip healed, I forgot about my attraction to my surgeon and just went on with my fast-paced career as a computer engineer. Today he is still tall, dark and handsome, but it is not the same. The passion has dissipated.

A couple of years ago I went back to him because my leg was hurting.

"Has anyone told you that you have an arthritic right knee?" Dr. Render said after his thorough examination of my right side. "You also need a revision on your artificial right hip. Otherwise, you look very good, very fit."

Not exactly good news, but something these remarkable surgeons can try to fix, so not entirely bad news either. If I do nothing, the prognosis is unthinkable: confined to a wheelchair or bedridden. I might as well jump off a cliff or have someone take me to a high mountain meadow and shoot me.

Handing me a physician's card he referred me to my new orthopedic surgeon at a fine hospital in south Denver.

This is where I am now, lying propped up in my hospital bed scribbling on a pad of paper.

The second definition for cougar, an attractive older woman who finds herself in a romantic relationship with a much younger man, is a better fit for this unusual story, in which the love interest is something much more than a man.

1.

Knee Replacement

The old passionate yearnings sprang to life again when my surgeon, Dr. Hess, met me in the hall at the hospital and asked me to walk with him during our first visit. This was the first time I had met my doctor. I had stopped at the restroom after my X-ray session, and as I exited, I sensed that I was being watched. Suddenly a man wearing a white lab coat appeared in an adjacent doorway.

"I'm Dr. Hess," he said. "Walk with me."

He had a fine reputation for being a world-class orthopedic surgeon. We began walking down the hallway when he said, "You are too young to be crippled like this."

His words were reassuring. At my age of 71 I wasn't getting any younger, so this was nice to hear. He stood aside and ushered me into an unadorned stark white room with an examining table and tall chair.

"Right here," he said graciously, holding the door as I entered the examining room. I looked sideways at him as I walked in, and noticed his eyes were a golden color and emitted golden flickers of light. His skin was suntanned a light bronze. He was broad shouldered and slightly stocky and an inch or two taller than I. I used to be 5 feet 8 inches tall, but with all my joint problems I have gotten shorter. He was light on his feet and gracefully muscular. Moving the door partially shut, his hand accidentally brushed my shoulder-length auburn hair. He smiled. I was captivated.

We talked for some time. He showed me my X-rays and carefully explained what had happened to me over the years. No other doctor had done that.

"You were born with a shallow right hip socket, and over time the socket became arthritic. Were you ever in an automobile accident?"

I shook my head no. He turned to face me. "Something must have triggered such wear and tear. As you know, the bad hip required an artificial implant, which, over the last 15 years, has now worn out. Your right knee is arthritic."

He paused for a moment then said, "I feel that I know you." He paused again and continued, "I know you came here expecting to schedule surgery for a second replacement of your right hip. We need to give you a right knee replacement first to stabilize the leg in order to support another new hip."

I was stunned. It seemed like there was a good distance between an arthritic knee and a complete knee replacement. I had not expected this. His eyes bore into mine. I quickly composed myself. "All right. When are you available?" I asked.

I sensed his approval at my quick decision. His gaze shifted from my face to the wall. More sparks sprang from his eyes. I could not read his expression, something I was usually good at. A guttural sound, almost a growl, came deep from his throat. His answer surprised me. He stood up, walked a few steps away from the examining table where I was sitting and said more to himself than to me, "Anytime. I am here all the time, even Saturdays."

A shadow fell over his profile and his face turned dark. His features became blurry, fur-like; his posture changed as his shoulders rounded. I was struck by the sadness in his voice. I had not thought I would hear such personal emotion from a famous surgeon. *This man is very weary and unhappy being confined within hospital walls,* I thought to myself. *There is a lot more to this man than is initially obvious.* I felt deep stirrings well up inside me—kinship, understanding, empathy, sadness, yearning, hope.

It was mid-March, early spring, and I told Dr. Hess that I had wanted to do many spring and summer plantings around my mountain home in Estes Park. "It is my new home and I really need to get the landscaping in."

"Okay, then," he said. "Enjoy your summer and let's plan on a late August surgery."

We agreed on August 26, and he said Glenda, his scheduling assistant, would handle the calendar and details.

Before leaving to go, I quickly asked him, "Can you give me a straight right leg?"

"Yes," he replied, "I can do that."

He quietly walked out the door not making a sound; feet slightly turned in; shoulders rounded. He did not say good-bye, nor did he look back. He just walked out soft footed and stealth-like.

The male cougar is a restless animal, as well as one of the fastest and most powerful of all the wild cats. The worst thing that can happen to him is to be caged. As a young adult he stakes out his area, which may be a wide circle of several hundred miles, and builds a den, which he visits occasionally. He is a loner but sometimes couples with a female cougar and can keep close to her for decades. A strong connection is often made when the female is injured or unable to care for herself. He doesn't go to her den but will take her to explore the territory he patrols. If he takes her to his den, he means to keep her as a mate with him for life.

On the way back home, I thought about what Dr. Hess had said about being in an automobile accident. Why was I so torn up? Then I remembered. About twenty years ago I had been in a motorcycle accident but had always believed I walked away unscathed. That event was a confusing time for me. Not long after the death of my husband and after a lot of insistence from a co-worker I got on the back of his big green motorcycle. It was a Friday afternoon before the Labor Day weekend and this was my first ride on a motorcycle—and my last.

I had been enjoying the ride: the freedom of feeling the air rush by; my long hair blowing loose from underneath the motorcycle helmet and wrapping around my neck. A few miles later, while stopped at a red light in the mountain town of Estes Park, we were rear-ended by a teenager driving his father's large pick-up truck. The teenager was traveling at about 30 miles per hour when he hit us, but even at that speed, the truck's wide bumper and grill were broken and caved in. The motorcycle was pushed into the intersection, as my co-worker's left leg and foot were pinned under the heavy motorcycle chassis, dragging him for a considerable distance. He almost lost his foot and it took him more than a year later to fully recover.

The young man who hit us from behind was not hurt and

said he was admiring the mountain scenery and had not seen us ahead of him, nor paid attention to the stoplight. It was a miracle that on that busy street we were not hit again sideways; but no traffic seemed to be present. I was thrown up in the air and landed on a grassy curbside beside the highway, yet I did not seem to get hurt at all. The doctor in the emergency room said it was a miracle I had escaped serious injury.

Before impact, I caught a glimpse of something tracking us from a distance, moving silently among the trees just beyond the grassy curbside knoll. The creature blended against the grey-tan colored bark of the aspen trees and brown trunks of the long-stemmed lodgepole pine trees. It moved swiftly and silently on four large paws. I was engrossed with the blurry movement in the trees and was totally unprepared from being hit from behind. I had no time to tense up or feel frightened.

I watched as the tan-colored cougar emerged from a stand of trees on the curbside knoll. He placed each large paw carefully on the grass, toeing in slightly, then stopped and looked directly at me: a handsome young male cat, strong and alert. Our eyes locked, and he held me suspended in the air. I felt him guiding me with his all-knowing, golden sparkling eyes.

As I sat upright and tried to orient myself, I took a bewildered look around me. The cougar was gone. Shortly after that, my sons gave me a poster, which I mounted next to a mirror above my bathroom sink. It was a picture of a young, tan-colored cougar hanging from a tree branch with the caption reading, "Hang in There, Baby!" The cougar looked like the one I had seen the afternoon of my motorcycle accident. Each morning as I was getting ready for work, I would touch the picture of the cat with my fingertips and thank him for saving my life. From that point on I felt an uncanny connection to Estes Park, and after retirement, I built a mountain home there.

Did the male cougar save my life and give me a premonitory warning of events to unfold? Was he still influencing me in ways I could not understand?

Native Americans believe if a male cougar enters your life he does so to teach you about your own power, about the crossroads in your life, and which direction you should follow.

Five months after my initial meeting with Dr. Hess and after I had worked on the landscaping of my new house, I returned in August for a pre-op visit before the knee replacement surgery. I was excited and nervous about this meeting. Would Dr. Hess hold such an attraction for me again? I tried to realign myself. Even though I am older than him, I am no dowdy, old woman. Before my recent retirement, I traveled the world supporting people in my role as CEO of my own software services company. Married and then widowed after more than thirty years and the mother of two outstanding young men, I had a proven track record of being a strong and capable woman.

Even though I was hurting, I did not want to look too pitifully crippled. I worked on my appearance in preparation for this meeting. My once pageboy-styled hair was now below shoulder-length and tinted a lighter auburn shade. I was immaculately dressed in dark brown cashmere slacks and a sweater. I might be broken, but I was not beaten. I was still hanging in there. How could this surgeon cause me to have butterflies in my stomach? As I waited for him in the examination room, I thought of his words at our first meeting: "I feel that I know you."

I whispered to myself, "He is also strangely familiar to me—his deep-set yellow eyes, his penetrating gaze. Where had I seen him before?" Dr. Hess and I met in the same stark examination room as my first visit: this time his medical assistant Davis was with him. I was disappointed that his assistant was there and we were not alone. Earlier that morning I had seen an internist in the hospital who had given me a nice compliment. "Biologically you are ten years younger than your age."

In addition to his routine examination I had an X-ray of my right hip and knee. Other tests had been taken:

blood samples, cardiogram (EKG) and chest X-ray. Dr. Hess had these results in his hand and he and Davis were reviewing them. We talked about my upcoming surgery and my general state of health.

"Your prognosis is good," Dr. Hess said, smiling widely. "You should do fine with this surgery. Besides, people who live in the mountains are a hardy lot."

Davis added, "He loves Estes Park and is always going there."

Both men sat side-by-side on the long examining table looking at each other as if they had secret stories to share. Their white lab coats spread out on each of their sides, their almost identical shiny black polished shoes not quite touching the floor. I sat in a tall chair opposite them. Both were fine-looking men with wide shoulders, narrow waists, muscular thighs and bulging zipper areas. They gazed at me steadily; they seemed almost like twins with deep-set, slanted yellow eyes.

As they left the room, Dr. Hess walked to my side and unexpectedly patted my shoulder. His hands were large and contoured. His nails were white and manicured. The hair on the back of his hands was long and golden in color. He bent toward me; did he like my perfume? He almost said something but then turned and left silently. I picked up his scent, a musky odor, wild and moist. I thought I heard a rumbling sound deep in his throat as he walked down the hall. Some might have thought he was just clearing his throat.

I had been losing the ability to walk any distance over the last few years. My case was complicated, because I had a bad right knee and a bad right hip. I was at the point where I could barely walk up my driveway after struggling to walk down to the mailbox, which was located on the street below my house. Getting the morning newspaper had become a daily chore, and I had to ask my neighbor if he would take the dumpster out on the road once a week for the trash pick-up. I loved working in my yard, but I had to scoot on the seat of my jeans or crawl on all fours to go up and down the banks to care for the flowers that encircled the house.

Even the act of driving had become difficult. My right knee would throb if I drove a few miles. Everything is controlled by the right leg in an automatic transmission car. It was now impossible to drive the 40 miles to see my oldest son and his family in the valley or to fly to see my younger son and his family in Seattle. I could hardly get myself to the grocery store and, for the most part, had to get everything delivered to the house. I was quickly becoming shut in, a recluse, and felt I was less sharp mentally. One of my friends said, "It's like losing yourself." This was true, but hard to hear. I wondered if I could keep living in my house, a home I had built with complete care and dedication and loved so much.

It wasn't fair what was happening to me. Three years ago I walked everywhere. I had always worked hard and exercised hard. In my twenties and thirties, I had climbed roughly half of the 14,000-foot mountains in Colorado. In my forties and fifties, I faithfully did aerobic dancing, Pilates and weight training. Then, in my late sixties, I started to fall apart physically. The medical literature on joint replacement advises not to have the surgery until you are so disabled there is no better recourse such as exercise, steroid shots, lesser surgery and painkillers. I thought I was at that point. I had to do something and I was ready.

The knee replacement surgery took place at noon on August 26. In the pre-operative surgery preparation area, my family stood around my hospital bed as I said good-bye to them. Smiles and hugs from everyone and then it was just me and my keepers.

"I'll see you afterward," I said with trepidation as they headed out the door. The anesthesiologist gave me a shot in the thigh and a shot in the spine at waist level.

"The shot in the spine blocks any sensation from the major nerves from the waist down," he explained. "The shot in the thigh blocks any sensation from the minor nerves and especially the sciatic nerve, which is very sensitive. The shot in the spine is called a femoral block and causes a temporary loss of the quadriceps' sensory and motor function. You will not be able to extend your lower leg or bear weight on that leg."

Even so, I imagined walking unassisted to the operating room. The nurse brought me back to reality as we walked the short distance down the lime-green hallway. I morbidly thought to myself, *Dead woman walking.*

"How do you look so young?" the nurse asked, interrupting my daydream. I don't think I answered, and I cannot remember going into the operating room. Was I on a gurney by then? Before the shots, my analytical brain had kicked in. I wanted to take in everything that was happening to me. I had wanted very much to see the operating room, how the medical team was preparing the room, the operating room bed (supposedly a weird looking piece of furniture that works well for operations but is anything but comfortable, however well padded), the instruments, and the coolness of the room. I had wanted to see Dr. Hess and his assistant in their scrubs. *Who else was in the operating room?* I thought to myself. *Would the lights be excruciatingly bright? Would there be music playing?*

I wondered why I was so much more interested in the

details of this surgery than I was 15 years ago when I had my total right hip replacement surgery. Maybe I was more frightened this time. The hospital had even requested a copy of my will when I checked in—not very reassuring.

With no memory of the operation, I also have no memory of the recovery room. I was told in the pre-op room that the nurse will check my blood pressure and respiration every 15 minutes. She will ask me my name and where I am, what surgery I have just had, to cough and take deep breaths, and check the condition of my legs and feet. Still, I cannot recall any of this. They didn't do that last time.

I remembered being wheeled on a gurney into my hospital room in the post-operative unit. My son, daughter-in-law and housekeeper, Tricia, were with me. My daughter-in-law commented on how lovely the room was. "You have a large window along the west wall. Look at the beautiful picture of Longs Peak on the south wall at the foot of your bed."

"Do you suppose they put you in this room because you have a view like this from your mountain home?" my son wondered.

"In fact," interjected Tricia, "this hospital is more like a fancy hotel than an inner-city hospital. We are going for a look around and have dinner in the bistro on the second floor after we leave you."

"Lucky you," I said sleepily. "Wish I were going with you."

My bed was placed parallel to the window so I could look out. I was hardly aware of my surroundings. I was fading in and out of consciousness, in a sleepy state due to the strong pain medicine I had been given. I realized that the nurse was checking the condition of my leg and checking my blood pressure, pulse and respiration.

"How much do you hurt?" she asked. "On a scale from one to ten how much pain are you feeling?"

In my pre-op visit I had been coached on what the pain scale means and how to judge my level of pain from one to ten, with ten being the worst.

"I'm about a six," I said.

The nurse went on. "If the medicine is not right for you, if it makes you sick to your stomach, we have something for this or we can ask your surgeon to try another pain medicine. Don't worry if you develop a slight itchy rash."

Immediately I felt the urge to scratch my leg. She again asked me to cough and breathe deeply. I breathed into a hand-held plastic device called an Incentive Spirometer. When breathing into it, a plastic ball is forced up into a graduated cylinder located in the middle of the device. The cylinder records how much air has been exhaled. If you can barely exhale it may mean you are developing pneumonia. The nurse adjusted cushion-like slippers on both of my feet. The slippers inflated and deflated with air, massaging my feet and legs. It sounded as if someone else was in bed with me breathing deeply, which I actually found comforting. She told me these are compression socks to keep the blood moving and to prevent clots from forming in the legs. I had been given a tablet of Coumadin (blood thinner) on the morning of my surgery to help reduce potential blood clotting.

I turned slightly onto my left side and watched the shadows of tree limbs moving in a light breeze outside my window. Golden afternoon sunlight filtered through the leafy branches, which were silhouetted against the burnt orange and rose reflections of the late afternoon sun. I felt dreamy. The scene reminded me of a Japanese landscape, and I immediately wished I were in Japan—anyplace but here.

As the nurse started to leave, she said, "This evening we will have you sit, stand and even walk. Exercise is very important."

How totally unrealistic, I wanted to say to her. *I can't even keep my eyes open.* Late that afternoon I sat on the edge of the bed and with the nurse's help, I stood up, took a few steps, then gratefully returned to bed. I was able to drink a cup of bouillon and felt buoyed up because my leg looked pretty good except for a red, 5-inch incision over my right knee held together by staples. My pain was at a level two; I had made it this far and my hopes were running high.

An hour later, in the dusky blue light of early evening, I heard people talking and walking back and forth in front of my door. I continued to doze and awaken in short intervals. The door of my room moved slightly and I saw two shadowy figures peer in, then leave. The room was almost dark except for two nightlights plugged into floor-level electrical outlets. I awakened to see a man in a white lab coat standing at the side of my bed. At first I was barely awake and did not recognize him. His face sagged somewhat and a short layer of yellow stubble was showing on his cheeks and chin.

"Hi, it's Dr. Hess. The surgery went very well. There were no surprises. This has been a good day."

He turned to look out my window.

"The other night," I started to speak. "I saw you on TV—Channel 7—taking some of your former joint replacement patients on the strenuous Grays and Torres peaks climb."

He brightened up. "You will be able to do that too," he said. Then he seemed hesitant. With even more surgery in my future, will that be true?

I replied quickly, "Oh, I have climbed both peaks in my past." His eyes looked deep into mine. "Distant past," I added.

I wanted him to know that even if I could never climb again I knew the fun of climbing high mountains and have experienced the enjoyment that he shared with his patients.

He stood in the middle of the large window in my hospital room and looked down on the courtyard. I sensed the tiredness and restlessness in the man. He had a full day of surgery and longed to be outside. I drifted into my drug-induced stupor for a short moment then again opened my eyes. I saw Dr. Hess walk to one side of the window and open it. Fresh night air blew across the bed. The tree branches outside seemed to move faster with the flowing breeze.

The sky was now jet-blue black. I dreamt that he crouched and sprang through the large window and into the darkness. I turned farther on my left side and could clearly see him walking around the courtyard below my window. Low border lights illuminated a grouping of rocks and shrubbery arranged in a circular pattern. He tore off his clothes and shoes and left them in a careless pile by a rock.

Effortlessly, the male cougar sprang up and rested upon one of the larger boulders. He stretched his long muscular limbs and extended his paws. Then he lay on his back, tucked his curled tail between his legs, folded his large paws across his belly and looked up at the star-studded sky. The long-nosed cat's face softened, his jowls slackened and he slept.

The male cougar, like the domestic male cat, assumes different positions when he is resting. If the cat rests on his back with paws folded across his body, this is a posture he assumes in preparation for a deep sleep. He is in his element, his belly is full, he feels secure. He is content, happy with himself and satisfied with the activities of his day.

When I woke early the next morning I dismissed the visions I saw the previous night as a drug-induced dream and quickly began preparations for the new day—day one (surgery day is considered to be day zero). The big event of the morning was taking a shower and dressing in my own gown and robe, which I had brought from home. I had not had much to eat since 6 P.M. the evening before my surgery and was starving. I devoured my breakfast of scrambled eggs, fruit and coffee in minutes. Getting back into bed after my shower I felt weak as a kitten and promptly threw up my entire breakfast on the newly sheeted bed. The nurse and physical therapist stood near my bed aghast at the mess I had made. They handed me a wet washcloth and towel.

"Here you go," the nurse said, handing me a wet washcloth and towel. "Please clean yourself up and put your soiled clothes in a plastic bag."

"Can we have the hospital laundry wash these clothes?" I asked, as I started to clean up my mess and change my clothes.

"No, you will just have to take them home with you and wash them there."

The hospital personnel seemed reluctant to clean up my vomit. Perhaps in today's environment—MESA, AIDS and swine flu viruses—they are fearful of patients' bodily fluids? For a fancy hospital, room service was mediocre. My once buoyant mood vanished, and I longed to be back at home with my garden and my cats.

The last time I felt this low was after my first visit with Dr. Hess in early March. My housekeeper, Tricia, drove me 70 miles for the appointment. We were in an exuberant mood driving down the canyon and into the valley. We talked about our favorite TV shows and movies and vowed to take more time off in the coming summer months for fun and relaxation. This is a typical reaction for people who live at high elevations. Living through a long winter season with so much snow and ice, one looks forward to warmer weather and savoring each warm day.

This time, our mood driving back home was different. Dr. Hess told me I needed a knee replacement as well as a hip revision. All I could imagine ahead of me were hospital stays, major surgeries and lengthy recovery times.

When Tricia dropped me off at home, she said, "Now I don't want you to fall into a major depression from all of this. You will do fine. Dr. Hess said you would. Want to see a movie next week?"

I nodded weakly and walked with great difficulty into the house.

A couple days later I began to research about what is involved with knee replacement surgery. It felt like going back to my high school biology days, reading about the basic structure and function of the knee off a medical site on the Internet:

The knee is the largest joint in the body. It consists of three parts: the lower end of the thighbone or femur, the upper end of the shin bone or tibia and the kneecap or patella. These three structures plus connective tissue and muscles work together. The patella slides on a groove on the end of the femur. Large ligaments attach the femur to the tibia to provide stability. The long thigh muscles give the knee strength. The joint surfaces where the three bones touch are covered with articular cartilage, a smooth substance that cushions the bones and enables them to move easily. All remaining surfaces of the knee are covered by a thin, smooth tissue liner called the synovial membrane. This membrane releases a special fluid that lubricates the knee, reducing friction to nearly zero in a healthy knee.

For some reason, when I thought about surgery on the leg, the first vision I had was of doctors in the Revolutionary War, amputating the leg of a poor wounded soldier with a hatchet and a saw without any anesthesia, except maybe a couple swigs of whiskey—and the patient screaming until he passes out. I forced myself to follow through with my investigation on the Internet, finding a website that showed step-by-step videos detailing the procedure.

"Do I really have to know anything about the procedure?" I inquired to myself. "Perhaps I should wait until after I have had the surgery."

I kept reading and became transfixed by what I was learning. "Total knee replacement surgery is fairly straightforward. The key to success is having a good knee prosthesis that can function as well as the original three parts of the knee."

Who were they kidding? I thought to myself. *I am no stranger to artificial parts—the right hip, a tooth implant, even contact lenses—and I know the artificial part is never as good as the original one I was born with.* I was halfway through the animated video—at the part where the surgeon uses a chisel to cut and shape the bones of the tibia, femur and patella. These bones are shaped to make room for the implants and to cut off diseased portions of the bone and cartilage, which, in my case, was osteoarthritis.

I had had enought and shut off the computer. Perhaps months later I would investigate further.

Turning back to the present, it was the morning of my first full hospital day. I thought about what my grandson Tommie had said earlier, "They will have to tear you down first in order to build you up."

My afternoon physical therapist, a large man, wheeled in a contraption that I was told is a Continuous Passive Motion Machine (CPM). I would come to refer to this wretched device as a torture rack as it bends and straightens the knee through all of the various degrees of knee bending while keeping the patient partially still on their left side. I found the last tight rotational bends of my knee (knee bends up to 120 degrees) was particularly painful. The physical therapist said that if I could endure these sessions, the proper functioning of my knee long-term will be assured. He would give me more pain medicine if necessary. I was strapped to the machine for two, 30-minute intervals with an hour break in between. Each time, I felt like a slave working beyond my limits. I was told that I would have to endure a final session tomorrow, to which I limply responded "I'll try."

I had turned down more pain medication in between the CPM sessions because the pain meds were making me feel weird. Perhaps tomorrow I should ask for more.

After my time on the torture rack I developed severe

gas pains. The night nurse came in that night with a long needle. I was terrified at the sight of such a long needle and knew that the injection would be excruciating. "This will reduce the gas," she said, then shot some medicine directly into my abdomen. Thankfully the shot hardly hurt at all and did eliminate my gas pains.

In the quiet, late afternoon that next day I began to think about everything that had happened over the last couple days. I started to daydream about the mysterious events I had experienced the night before. My thoughts were interrupted by a sound at my door. In the twilight I saw a shadow in my doorway. Someone was watching me. As he turned to leave, I saw golden flickers of light emitting from his eyes.

"We must keep close tabs on her," I heard him say to someone behind him. "She is exhausted and frightened. Her blood pressure is dropping." His voice was full of concern.

"I hope it is Dr. Hess who is talking," I whispered to myself, "because I think I need his help."

The male cougar has won the respect of all the other animals in his neighborhood. He is fearless in his endeavors and will not stop unless he is successful or dead. He is a mighty hunter and a cunning strategist. He plans every detail of his work. He is one of the few animals that can kill a porcupine without sustaining injury to himself. He knows how to quickly flip the porcupine on his back and skillfully rip the soft underbelly. He moves in rapid spurts and leaps and at times appears to be flying. He has very keen eyesight and is agile and sure-footed. He learns in increments with rest periods in between. He does not accept failure easily.

2.

Cougar Flight

The night nurse came back into my room. "He's always checking on you," she said.

I didn't know what she meant and asked, "Who?"

She answered with some irritation in her voice, "Dr. Hess."

I thought to myself, *I bet she is stuck on him. Nurses always have crushes on their doctors, especially successful, good-looking ones.* I blushed, realizing, of course, that I too had a crush on him.

She had me sit up and breathe into the spirometer. She took my blood pressure and temperature. "We are going to try another pain medicine. We think your present pain medicine is making you feel strange and also making your blood pressure drop."

I have read up on pain medications and reviewed

what I knew. There are essentially two kinds of painkillers or analgesics: narcotic and non-narcotic. The narcotic painkillers are more effective for moderate to severe pain and can be used safely for the short term. Over the long term, they can make the patient physically and neurologically dependent on them. Then you turn into a raging addict, which seems horrific to me. I would rather suffer than end up like that.

I knew a woman who has been on painkillers for over a year after a total knee replacement. I have made the determination not to take pain medication for longer than four weeks. I found out later that another good reason for limiting the length of painkiller use is because the longer you used it the first time, the less effective that particular painkiller is the next time you need it. In other words, your body "remembers" this drug and blocks its usefulness later on.

Dr. Hess prescribed a narcotic painkiller for me, a special-blended, semi-synthetic type of opioid consisting of acetaminophen and hydrocodone. Acetaminophen is what is found in Anacin, Excedrin and Tylenol. Hydrocodone, a compound derived from codeine, is the narcotic part. At the end of day one, the medical staff thought I must be reacting to the codeine. I was not doing well on this blended painkiller and they wanted to try another narcotic. This was distressing. The painkiller was suppressing the normal rhythms of my intestinal tract, and I was suffering from severe cramping and constipation, which is why I had a long needled shot to the abdomen. Two of the biggest challenges after major surgery are to effectively control pain and prevent constipation. Both situations are bad for the patient if not promptly treated, not to mention making your life thoroughly miserable.

The night nurse changed my hospital gown, which I had soaked through as a result of my profuse perspiring. I had started to shake and break out in cold sweats. She placed another blanket on top of me and exited the room.

Dr. Hess and Davis suddenly appeared by my bedside. They talked earnestly to each other then turned to me.

"We will help you," Dr. Hess said. "You will be okay. You are a strong woman."

He turned to Davis and said more softly, "She will try hard to make a success of our efforts."

I heard only part of the rest of what they said—something about allergic reaction to the pain meds, feeling frightened and overwhelmed. I wondered, *Is that what they think has been making me so sick?* I tried to think through all of this and must have dozed, because when I awoke, it was pitch black outside. The night nurse walked in and Dr. Hess, who was at my bedside, told her that he would take care of things, that he would stay with me. She walked out briskly, somewhat irritated, her black pumps making a sharp slap on the linoleum floor with each step.

The cushion-like slippers on my feet were gently pushing air back and forth, and the breathing sounds of the air compressor comforted me. I then felt someone turning me onto my left side. Dr. Hess perhaps? Something warm and fluffy was tucked around my back as tropical air circulated around my neck, back, shoulders and legs. Deep breaths, hot breaths, wet breaths. I was feeling cared for and felt no pain. A golden glow of pleasure irradiated through me—plumping, moist, erotic. I felt soothed and comforted. I felt myself drifting off to sleep with the sensation of someone—or something—lying behind me, breathing deeply, massaging my neck and shoulders in wide, circular, soft, furry paw strokes. I heard a whirring, almost a purring in my ears. I hummed myself to sleep and awoke again several minutes later to a repeat of the same sensations.

> When the male cougar is content he will stretch out his paws, knead the softness he is resting on and make purring sounds just like a domestic cat. He covets soft and warm surfaces and is known to make a soft bed for himself in his den using pine needles, dry leaves and animal fur. He is a tender lover and mates with his partner in a few rapid swift strokes and then rests to

begin again later. They rest together, his body wrapped around hers. Both cats purr themselves to sleep.

When I think we are awake and without saying a word, the cougar and I talk for a long time. I have no trouble understanding him although his voice is low and coarse. We talk telepathically, not speaking out loud.

"Why are you frightened?" the cougar asks.

I have thought about this and can answer right away. "It is not about my knee surgery. It is about the next surgery, the hip revision."

He leans closer to me. "Why are you so worried about it?"

"I have read about it. Supposedly, it is much more difficult than the first time the hip was replaced and because I will need bone grafting, the surgery is even more problematic."

He looks deeply into my eyes.

I can't seem to stop talking; I'm almost whimpering. "This all seems too much. Why go through all this to end up crippled and not able to walk after all? Or worse, I could die on the operating table."

The cougar assures me. "I will give you my best support. You will persevere, even thrive."

I object. "How can you be so sure? What do you know about me?"

He took a long time to think of his answer, then spoke. "Okay come with me. Walk with me."

We slid out of bed and he walked with me to the window of my hospital room. In one swift motion he opened the window and took my hand with his paw, swinging me onto his back.

"We will fly part of the way and then we will walk," he said. "I want to show you something."

As we exited the window, I immediately noticed that night had turned to day with the sun directly overhead, shining brightly in my face. I had to shut my eyes; the light was so bright. We were high in the sky over the Denver skyline, heading west to the silver-capped Rocky Mountains beyond. The cougar moved with silent grace, strength and ease, as I gripped his fur, clinging tightly to his back. In what seemed like a few seconds, I saw that we were entering Estes Park and approaching the intersection where I was hit by the truck so many years ago.

"Do you remember this place?" he asked.

He showed me images of the accident, as if it were a movie being projected onto the bright sky. I saw my landing on the grassy knoll near the intersection.

"You should have died there," the cougar said, "but I was able to save you. I knew you would need my help then and in the future. Rest assured, I will help you recover from your crippled joints."

We turned to leave and he flew me over my home in Estes Park. We circled the house twice as I held tightly to his back.

"I thought you might want to see your home," he said. "Perhaps you are homesick? Tomorrow will be your last day in the hospital; then you will go home to recover. The landscaping looks good. I watched you work on your yard last summer. That was when you were crawling on all fours up and down the banks of your property. You won't have to do that much longer. I have a den over the hill."

I remembered how my grandsons and I saw a cougar sunning himself on a rock on the mountain behind my house.

"That must have been you then?" I asked him.

"Yes, and I was the cougar who greeted you the morning after you moved in."

I never forgot that morning. We were living in the part of the house that had been completed. I got up early and was feeding my four domestic cats when I decided to open the door that was leading to a large, deep hole we had excavated for the next stage of our building. It was barely light out. As I opened the door with my cats lined up behind me in their customary manner, directly below us in the open pit was a beautiful cougar with sparkling golden eyes gazing at us. My cats hissed, and I slammed the door so hard the transom window above the door quivered. I was sure the cougar was preparing to leap and kill us with his swift, long paw-clawed blows.

"I was just checking on you," the cougar said. After I saved you on the grassy knoll I could not let you go. I have been with you for a long time. My clan has designated me to be your tutelary spirit and protector."

The male cougar rarely chooses a mate for more than one season, yet there are instances when he will stay with a mate who is injured and unable to protect herself—even stay from year to year. He is very selective about choosing his mate and with the help of his clan, often chooses a mature mate years older than he to be his partner. It is imperative for him to find a mate who can match his mental and emotional faculties. His goal in life is to seek knowledge, and he wants to learn from her.

On the way back to the hospital, riding high up on the cougar's back, I confided to him that my fearfulness was more than just fear of crippled joints and surgery.

"Before my conversation with you this evening I felt terribly alone," I told him. "My sons are grown up and very busy with their own families. I'm lucky to talk with them twice a month. No one seems to have time for me."

"That is the way of the animal kingdom here on earth,"

said the cougar. "Families change as the children grow up. They are supposed to leave their parents and make their own lives. You did a good job with your sons. The way they are now, you were too at their age. Now is the time for you to have a new and freer life. You are the one to determine what happens next. Living life is like peeling an onion. You move down the onion layer by layer, and the closer you get to the center, the sweeter it becomes if you have the resolve to thrive, to endure the pain of the tears, and if you have the good health to enjoy it."

The male cougar is an indifferent parent. He ignores his offspring and will chase them away when they are old enough to make it on their own. Yet, he keeps tabs on them, sometimes for years—and will circle their dens and let them know of his presence before he moves on.

It was early morning just before dawn when we arrived back at the hospital. We sat together, side-by-side, on the outcropping of rocks just below my hospital window. I finally got up the nerve to ask him the question I had wanted to ask since we first met.

"How can you be both a man and a cougar?"

He spoke in a calm, controlled voice, again through my

mind. "The short answer is that I have learned to tap into the creature inside me to access those abilities that would be hard for a man to do alone. Everyone has these powers, but few ever develop them. They might have glimmers of this power, but the awareness soon passes. Inside each of us is a creature. The creature is part of the person and is a particular animal of the same DNA as the person. You and I have the same DNA. We are soul mates. We are both cougars. This inheritance goes back to the beginning of time. You have heard of the primitive brain?"

I nodded.

"Well there's a lot more to it than most people realize. I had reached a plateau in my surgery where I could not achieve the very best results that I wanted. I just wasn't skilled enough. I had to find a way and I did. When I was completing my medical specialty after medical school I studied with a learned medical doctor from the Himalayas. He trained me to tap into these special powers, to give me the strength and endurance to perform the surgeries that I now do, and to instill in my patients the ability to realize their own true powers. I have extremely steady hands and can manage the various tools that I need to cut bone, put in an artificial prosthesis, and do heavy lifting as I am operating. Being an orthopedic surgeon takes a lot of strength. Some of my peers use a system of ropes and pulleys to lift limbs and reposition the patient during surgery. I think that can cause bruising, even injury. I do all the work by hand, unassisted by machines, and my patients recover quickly. Most of my patients have reached a point in their lives, almost like jumping off a cliff, where they must determine what direction to take, either to be crippled or whole."

"What about Davis?" I ask him. "He seems to have these special gifts too."

"Yes, Davis is one of my disciples, a member of my clan. He will be a great surgeon."

The cougar looked tired. "I must quickly tell you a few things and then go to prepare for a long day of surgery tomorrow."

He began to tell me how it was his job to show me my special, inner power. "You have the ability to forge a very good life for yourself. Twenty years ago you were at a crossroads when you were hit by the truck. Shortly after that, because you felt stuck in your work, you were able to change jobs and better yourself. You put your sons through college, kept your home and improved it, and retired successfully, even well liked. You built a retirement home in the mountains, something you had always wanted to do. Now you must prepare for the next decade. Your new challenge is to get your worn-out joints replaced. You were courageous to take this step to have a knee replacement. It shows you are brave and have plans for the future. You will be courageous and successful in having a hip revision next fall. Use the wisdom that you have gathered over the years and choose your friends and activities wisely. Experimenting and dabbling in many endeavors is appropriate when you were young but not now. Be selective. Always know that I will be with you."

He then asked me, "What have you learned over the last few years? What are your interests?"

"I want to write," I replied. "I came to Estes Park to write about what I know. Writing is something I have always wanted to do, but I had a professional career in the physical sciences that took most of my time and all of my energy. I don't care if I am a raging success as a writer; I just want to do it. I also want to garden, to have lots of beautiful plants and trees on the acre lot around my house. I want to keep my family and good friends close. I'm not a joiner and I am content to be alone for long stretches of time. I think I need time to be creative. I don't want to be sick and crippled."

The cougar smiled, golden flickers of light radiating from his eyes. I felt more at peace than I had in a long time.

His words kept ringing in my ears: "You and I have the same DNA. We are soul mates. We are both cougars."

I awoke to my darkened hospital room and saw Dr. Hess sitting in a chair near my bed. He noticed that I was awake and walked up to my bedside.

"I'm glad to see you are feeling better. You responded very well to the new pain medicine. Your temperature and blood pressure are normal. We had to wrap you in an air compression blanket cushion last night to stabilize your blood pressure and keep your temperature from dropping. We checked on your temperature several times during the night. We didn't want it to drop to a dangerous low level. You may have noticed the bright sunlamp we focused on you to warm you up quickly. Davis and I have taken turns watching you through the night."

I had recalled the feeling of warmth during the night.

Dr. Hess went on. "We're no longer worried now. You have remarkable stamina and have recovered quickly. It's about four in the morning, and the night nurse will be in to check on you. Davis will see you later in the afternoon. If you are still doing well you should be able to check out and go home before dinnertime. Of course, we will keep a close watch on you while you are home. We have some very good homecare nurses and therapists in Estes Park. As long as you are stable, I think the best healing occurs at home where there aren't so many interruptions."

I started to say something but only smiled. Doesn't he remember what we said and did last night? Dr. Hess lowered his shoulders and quietly exited my room, not saying anything, walking on soft paw feet, toeing in slightly. I couldn't make out a purring sound this time.

> The male cougar has great endurance, but when he tires he must crawl away and recharge himself. He will round his shoulders, tuck his head and creep away to a place where he can rest undisturbed. In addition to his main den, which is usually inside a cave of dirt and rocks, he also establishes temporary dens close to his hunting and eating areas.

3.

Soul Mates

I was able to endure the torture rack for 30 minutes in the late morning of my last day in the hospital. My knee did not pain me as much as it did yesterday, and the new pain medicine was working better.

As afternoon came on, thoughts turned to excitement over being able to go home. I had just taken a shower and washed my hair when Davis walked into my room. He complemented me on getting myself cleaned up, and joked with me about how he was glad I did not throw up all over him.

"You have made enormous strides today," he said. "I have your discharge papers. Most of your healing will take place while you are at home and especially over the next three to four months. It will take a good year or more for your knee to be totally healed. As soon as we have completed all this paperwork, you are free to go. We will have the visiting home nurse and physical therapist look in on you at your home tomorrow and then three times a week for a month."

He asked if I had any questions. I must have looked puzzled because he pulled up a chair next to my bed and continued, "Keep taking your pain meds until you no longer need them, but do space out the frequency of self-medication until you need only one tablet a day. You should do very well and we will call you in a few days and set up a one-month and two-month return visit for checkups. Don't hesitate to call us if you have any questions or problems." As he said this, his deep-set brown eyes sparkled golden flecks.

After Davis left the room, I moved to start gathering my personal things from the closet near the end of my bed, including the plastic bag full of vomited clothes. I carefully gathered the notes I had written on pieces of tablet and stuffed the sheets into my overnight bag.

I phoned Tricia. "I'm ready to go home now," I told her. "Please come and get me." She told me that Davis had called her before I did and she was already on her way.

My mood was the lightest it had been in weeks. I had confidence that I could walk out of my hospital room, down the hall and to the parking area outside the hospital pushing my walker. What a wonderful feeling to be walking again. I was on my feet and moving more surely than I had in a long time. My new knee had given me a new straight leg.

Time at home went from one productive day to the next with by-weekly visits by my physical and occupational therapists. Four weeks later we had reached an important goal: I was off pain medicine. I began to feel like my old self again. Tricia said that "The lady of the house has returned." I hadn't thought much more about my cougar and was sure this was only my imagination. Over the next two months though, Tricia and I occasionally saw a male cougar circling my home.

The male cougar is protective of his mate. He will check on her periodically and makes plans for their next encounter. With sure-footed stealth and use of his knowledge of camouflaging himself behind rocks and trees, he can remain out of her sight. If she sees him, he means to be visible.

In the spring of 2010, almost ten months after my knee replacement, my oldest son, Dan, picked me up at my home in Estes Park and drove me 70 miles to the hospital in South Denver. I was scheduled to see Dr. Hess. I eased into the passenger seat of Dan's Honda Accord, protecting my right hip as much as possible. Dan smiled and teased me as we pulled out of my wide driveway.

"Another surgery, mom," he said, turning to me with a wide grin. "What a bummer! So ... to ease this stress, we are going out for a fine lunch after we see your doctor."

I patted Dan's knee. I wanted our conversation in the car to be about anything but my health. I never liked it when people talked endlessly about their medical problems, and now I found myself doing it!

On the drive down the mountain canyon we talked about fun family times. But my mind worked in overdrive as I kept reflecting on my upcoming doctor's visit and tried to come to grips with what was going to happen.

As my thoughts wandered, I kept seeing visions of my orthopedic surgeon as the strong, buff-colored male cougar. I kept reminding myself that all of my memories and visions of the cougar and the closeness we felt were only hallucinations. Tricia thought differently. She is part Native American and believes in the oneness and powers of animal spirits. What if she is right? What if I see the cougar again when I look into the eyes of my surgeon? Of course you won't, I told myself, shaking my head. That time you were heavily drugged. Aside from Tricia, I had told no one else about these visions.

The moment I walked into Dr. Hess's office, the surgery

became incidental to me. Maybe I should not have come back. Maybe I should have found another orthopedic surgeon. Maybe I'm just a silly, even crazy, woman. Yet, I was convinced he was the only doctor who could heal me—he and the cougar within him.

Sunlight streamed in from a small window above the examination table, illuminating Dr. Hess's honey-colored, golden hair, as he entered the room behind his assistant, Davis. He touched me lightly on the shoulder as he walked by. I turned, and he looked directly into my eyes. Time seemed to stop for both of us. The animal attraction and personal connection were still there.

Dr. Hess looked older and thinner, the bony structure of his brow and cheeks were more pronounced. He was not as tan as he was last fall, and white hairs were visible around his ears and forehead. His shoulders were more rounded than I had remembered. His expression was still one of strong resolve, but he seemed constrained, caged in, by his relentless over-worked, over-stressed hospital life. His once slanted amber eyes, which emitted gold sparks as he talked, were now set deeper and were lighter in color—almost blue against the light blue wall of his office. His voice was lower and came deeper from within his broad chest.

I remembered what he had said last time, "We are both cougars. We have the same DNA. We are soul mates."

He moved to a corner of the room where he sat legs apart, head erect, crouched on a chair beside the examination table and next to Davis. His white lab coat parted, and I could see his immaculately pressed tan gabardine trousers, his pale blue dress shirt and the attractive blue and gold silk tie meticulously tied at his neck. As he shifted position, I could clearly see the form of a cougar. His movements, gestures, and poses fascinated me, and his proud head, broad nose, and deep-set eyes added to this vision.

Davis did the customary greetings and displayed my latest hip X-ray on the monitor, which sat on a small table beside us. Even though Dr. Hess began to speak in a well-modulated voice, I had a hard time concentrating on his words. I wanted to stand by his side and touch him, run my fingers through his thick hair, pat his head, stroke his nose, caress and kiss him, encourage him to break free from this small room. Most of all, I wanted to leave with him.

Native Americans knew that as the cougar ages, his fur loses some of the fawn-colored undercoat, darkens, toughens and eventually whitens. His fur becomes more bristle-like around the nose and mouth. The eyes become lighter in color and set deeper into his eye orbs. His face lengthens and becomes chiseled with each feature more well-defined beneath a heavily ridged brow. Aging can occur rapidly after his twentieth year and is an individual matter dependent on how hard his life has been. A male cougar can live forty years or more.

Dr. Hess began to describe his plans for repairing my hip.

"I know just what we must do before there is more damage to the hip area." He again looked directly at me. "The polymer lining of the hip joint from the old joint replacement is flaking off, which is causing you pain and weakening the muscles, tendons and connective tissue. Have you noticed how unsteady your gait is?"

Dr. Hess then explained that the ball of my hip joint moved laterally with each step. The ball slips within the worn-out socket, giving me an unsteady gate. My new knee was trying to stabilize my leg, doing both the work of a hip and a knee, and was having a hard time.

I murmured, "I wondered why I felt that I might fall down at any moment."

All of us were quiet for a few moments. Then Dan shifted in his chair and spoke directly to Dr. Hess.

My son did not seem to see the cougar and asked, "Why is the polymer flaking off?"

Dr. Hess looked down. "Back when your mother had her primary hip replacement, a polymer was used to line the hip socket. Before placement in her body, the polymer was irradiated to kill bacteria. Now we know that radiation causes the polymer to disintegrate over time, probably from pressure and friction within the joint. At that time, the polymer lining was considered a wonderful innovation to help the hip joint move smoothly. We have now replaced this with a much safer plastic lining."

He paused.

Davis spoke up, "Yes, our joint replacements are getting better every year."

Dr. Hess added, "Davis will give you more information about the operation and what to expect."

Having said what he came to say, Dr. Hess looked down at his watch. A strand of hair fell over one of his eyes. He stood up quickly and stretched his back, leg and neck muscles. I observed each detail. The cougar was trying to break free. Dr. Hess, a man who was not prone to acknowledging silly remarks, wanted to leave the confines of the small examining room.

Still stunned by seeing a cougar again, I found myself stuttering, "I … I hope you do a good job on my h-hip." I felt I needed to say something to bring myself back to reality. My voice sounded high pitched and child-like. Why would I say that?

He lifted his head and in a rough, almost inaudible voice said, "I did a great job with your knee, didn't I?" He looked down at his feet. I heard a rumbling sound from deep within his throat as he turned his head. Was he scolding me?

Around his lips I noticed individual hairs starting to stiffen, the once-yellow hairs now turning white. Without pausing, he left the room, shoulders hunched, head slightly bent, toeing in as he padded down the hall on his crepe-soled shoes.

Native Americans had witnessed mature male cougars breaking free from imprisonment: at first looking down at the ground while planning his strategy for escape, stretching his body to its full length, giving forth restless deep sounds from his throat and finally breaking free with a quick and mighty lunge. He is more often than not successful in his escape because, in addition to his cunning, he has exceptionally powerful neck, shoulder and leg muscles.

Davis took up the topic of painkillers because I had trouble after my last surgery with the codeine, opium-based pills they had prescribed.

"We are prescribing a new painkiller for you this time. It is Tramadol and is highly effective—hopefully no more hallucinations."

I asked if I would be taking Coumadin again.

Davis answered, "Yes, Wafarin, commonly known as Coumadin, a blood thinner. We are always concerned about blood clots forming, especially with hip surgery."

Davis continued, "As to the actual operation itself, you have to have this hip revision because the old artificial hip has worn out, as you know. Revision hip replacements are more complicated and the outcomes are not as good as a first hip replacement.

Dan interrupted. "But aren't hip replacements getting better and easier every year?"

"Yes, but hip revisions are a little trickier. Technical problems include the quality of the bone and the ability to secure the revision hip replacement parts into position. Removing the old parts may require more extensive surgery."

"I'm not trying to scare you, just inform you," Davis said, "Often blood loss is considerable, and you may have to have a blood transfusion and bone grafting. Because of these factors, revision surgery is much more complex, which means a longer time in surgery, longer recovery and rehabilitation time, and later, poorer hip mobility."

Concerned, Dan and I looked at each other and then back to Davis, who continued, "Dr. Hess has carefully considered all of these factors and still believes that he can construct a new hip that will allow you to adequately recover."

The three of us sat in silence. Davis asked if we had any other questions, but we didn't. He shook our hands and we all left the room.

On the way out of the hospital, I stopped in the restroom. I was thinking about my poor physical condition and how much Dr. Hess had aged in the past year. The ladies' room was lined with mirrors, and I gasped. Was I that old woman reflecting back at me? I was hunched. I leaned forward as I walked. Even though I was not overweight (in fact I had lost weight), my stomach protruded. One shoulder was higher than the other. I really did not have a waist at all. What happened to me? Thanks to my hairdresser, my hair was cut in an attractive page-boy style and colored a dark auburn shade; but my face was gaunt and I had dark circles under my eyes. For months at home I had not taken a good look at myself. The only mirrors I have are over the bathroom sinks and reflect an image from chest height up.

At that moment, I realized that not only was major surgery an obstacle, but somehow I would have to reclaim my once-attractive figure, high cheek-boned face and maybe even my good mind. I had felt particularly dull lately. The mind might be the hardest to recapture. Was it too late? Did I have the physical and emotional strength to do all this?

"Not today," I told myself. "Maybe eventually with my cougar's help." I laughed out loud, a shattered sound like broken pieces of glass glittering off the shiny white tiles above the bathroom sink.

I walked out of the bathroom somewhat shaken. Dan was waiting for me at the nearby elevator that would take us to the ground level and out the main entrance. He turned to meet me with a warm smile and held my jacket. The sound of glass shards faded away.

Fortunately, Dan had parked at the hospital's ER entrance, only a short distance from the main entrance, which was helpful since I was having difficulty walking— more like shuffling and wobbling.

Back in the car, I pictured Dr. Hess before he exited the examination room, his head slightly bowed, not a glance at me, not a handshake, no good-byes. What did I expect?

I whispered to myself, "The cougar has broken free from the cage of the examining room. He could hardly wait to go." But he also had a set to his jaw, a look of determination and control that put me at ease. Even though I had been anxious after hearing details about the surgery, I now felt consoled and at peace. Dr. Hess was determined to make me better. I knew the hip revision surgery would go well. Yet, at the same time, I believed I was losing my mind. I had seen the cougar again and I was not on painkillers.

4.

Hip Revision

Months later, I was at home watching a television science program on the *Discovery* channel about parallel universes, the concept of living in two different places at one time with different lives and outcomes. I wondered if I had slipped into one of these realms with Dr. Hess. The program said that the theory of parallel universes or the "many worlds theory" is based on the Heisenberg Uncertainty Principle concerning photons or light particles. I remember studying this principle in college and being fascinated by it. The photon can exist in a particular form or state (wave or particle of light) in two places at the same time. And this is the part that really startled me: the photon's existence depends on its choosing.

I like to have an understanding about the things I'm learning and want answers to situations that don't make sense to me. Perhaps quantum physicists have discovered something very important with this theory. I believe it can explain the behavior of sub-atomic particles, but I don't think that this applies to people in the here and now. At any rate, I did not *choose* to see a cougar as my surgeon and with strong resolve will make sure it doesn't happen again. In a few weeks, when I am scheduled to see Dr. Hess for a checkup, I planned to be better prepared— physically robust and mentally sharp. Sooner than I had planned I had a chance to test my resolve.

It was six months after my hip revision surgery. Dr. Hess and I were trapped in my mountain home by a relentless, once-in-a-century blizzard on a bleak day. The date was Friday, November 19, a day that would later go down in the record books as sustaining the heaviest snowfall ever recorded in the region. The time was 8 P.M., and we were ensconced in my mountain home after just barely making it back from a local restaurant a few blocks away.

A lot had happened since early that morning when Dr. Hess's assistant Glenda called and said, "There is no need for you to come all the way to South Denver for your six-month hip revision checkup next week. Let's see …"

Her voice faded for a moment as I heard a rustling of papers. "... er ... Monday, November 22 ... that was the date scheduled for your next appointment, right? Dr. Hess will be in Estes Park today. He can see you later this afternoon."

"Why is he in Estes Park?" I inquired.

"He is giving a seminar this morning to a group of Rocky Mountain orthopedic surgeons," she said. "A new ortho wing is being constructed at the hospital in Estes Park."

I murmured something about being happy to hear that and after a pause she said, "This afternoon he has three patients to see—you, if that will work, and two others." The sound of shuffling papers came over the phone receiver. "Hmmm ... he can see you at 3:00 P.M. in room 204 in the main building of the hospital."

By 11 A.M. on that infamous Friday the snow began sifting down slowly. As is typical of mountain weather, we had varying periods of snowfall, bright sun and blue sky, low-hanging clouds and then a low swollen sky about ready to burst with heavy snow. By 12:30 P.M. I was getting worried. I called Glenda and told her I would have to cancel because I could not drive to the hospital on account of it snowing so hard. Snow doesn't usually bother me but I could see this was cranking up to be a major storm. After three joint replacements I was more careful about getting stranded and I knew there was no way I would be able to walk my way out.

Fifteen minutes later Glenda called me back, "Dr. Hess says not to worry. He will pick you up at your home. He is driving his black four-wheel-drive Cadillac Escalade, so it does great in snow. He'll pick you up around 1 P.M."

I felt anxious and excited about being with Dr. Hess again, particularly being alone with him in an environment outside the hospital. I also wanted to show him my new mountain home, my pride and joy. I carefully showered, shampooed, dried my hair and stepped into dark blue silk slacks, a white silk blouse and black leather boots. I looked in the full-length mirror and thought, *I look good; I think I can outwit any cougar!*

A little while later, I heard his Escalade drive up my long driveway, followed shortly by his footsteps on the porch and opened the front door. I was not nervous at all; just glad to see him. "Hi, Dr. Hess, thanks so much for picking me up. I really appreciate this."

He smiled broadly at me. "Hi, nice to see you again."

"Well, please come on in," I said. "This is quite some storm we're getting."

"Sure is," he said as he stepped into the foyer area and stomped the snow off his boots, brushing the snow off his shoulders of his light blue wool sweater (he wasn't wearing a coat), ruffling the snow out of his hair.

"If you have a few moments I'd like to show you my new

home."

"Thanks, but we'll have to leave right now because my first appointment is in fifteen minutes."

"Oh, that's okay," I said, feeling slightly foolish and dejected.

"I can't seem to stick to a schedule today. Perhaps I'll have time to see your lovely home when we return?"

"Yes, that would be great."

I went to the entryway closet to retrieve my coat. He graciously helped me slip it on and shut the front door behind us. We walked several feet along the driveway to his car. Dr. Hess commented on the large trees on both sides of the drive way. He said he appreciated these big trees and especially the massive one closest to us. He stopped walking and stood in my driveway with his arms outstretched, like he was trying to embrace its girth. "That tree is enormous."

"Yes," I said, "several trees are over two hundred years old. This one, the one you especially like, is my 'Raggedy Ann' tree. She is four hundred fifty years old."

Dr. Hess turned in a circle trying to get the best view of her. When I told him how old "she" was, he agreed, exclaiming, "That old girl is one of the biggest and most beautiful in Estes Park."

The driveway was rapidly filling in with snow and I hoped that Tommie, my snow removal guy, would clear it off while we were gone. As I took a big step up to get into the leather passenger seat of his Escalade, Dr. Hess stood behind me to help me get in and shut the heavy car door. He pointed up to the sky. "Look above. A large flock of birds! They are in a hurry, wanting to fly south and get out of the cold weather."

"What a great flock. I think they are blackbirds," I surmised.

Our short drive to the hospital from my house took longer than we had anticipated because we had to wait for a large herd of elk to cross the road in front of us. A few moments later we saw a herd of deer huddled under thick evergreen foliage.

Dr. Hess said, "I have been seeing deer and elk massing together all along my drive in Estes Park today. I think they are anticipating a big storm."

It was 1:15 P.M. when we entered the orthopedic area in the hospital's new west wing. Except for my checkup with Dr. Hess I didn't see him the rest of the afternoon. The time at the hospital came and went with a blur: many different conversations, many different footfalls. I sat for a long stretch of time in an interior waiting area reading magazines and walking down the long hallway admiring the patterns of carpeting and tiles on the hospital floors. It was a relief to see Dr. Hess finally walk toward me at 4:30 P.M. He looked tired but smiled at me as he put on his jacket.

We walked out of the hospital into a blinding snowstorm. High winds drove the flour-like snowflakes across our faces, pushing horizontally across the glow of the large parking lot lights and the lanterned pathway before us. Large evergreen trees around the hospital's parking lot projected dark shadows in front of us like capped sentinels guiding our way to the car.

"I didn't know all this was happening outside," I said.

He laughed softly, a sound coming deep from within his chest. "I've been so busy inside I forgot about the weather."

As we got into his car, Dr. Hess said, "I'm starving. I think we should stop at a nearby inn."

"That would be very nice," I said. "I'm getting pretty hungry."

"I know of this old rustic inn close to your house, and I know the owner and the chef. He cooks a wonderful filet mignon. I've had very little to eat since my 4:30 A.M. breakfast at home in Denver."

"Sure, of course," I nodded my head in agreement, shaking the snowflakes off auburn hair and eyelashes.

"I know the inn. They serve wonderful French onion soup in this homemade bread bowl." That, plus a glass of red wine, would be a wonderful addition to the cold, snowy weather around us.

"I'm also famished and feel rather tired and weak," I said in an almost inaudible tone.

Dr. Hess turned and looked at me with his penetrating, golden-flecked eyes. "I'm not surprised. The post-op hip checkup is long and detailed, and you had quite a wait this afternoon while I checked on my other patients. Feeling tired is normal, but you are healing up magnificently just like you did after your knee surgery."

Suddenly the weather improved. The snowflakes slowly filtered down and clouds parted to reveal a steel gray sky with wispy clouds. The sun was setting fast, appearing like a large hazy magenta orb on the skyline.

"Typical mountain weather," Dr. Hess, said jokingly, "One minute a blizzard and the next moment, spring. The heavy snowfall will no doubt return when it gets dark."

Navigating the icy roads we made it to the inn without difficulty. We entered through the large double-doored entrance, and a man whom Dr. Hess called Roscoe met us.

"Dr. Hess, we are so glad you can dine with us tonight. I'll tell Mary when I get home that the surgeon who saved her life was here."

"Give my best to Mary," Dr. Hess said with a smile as he shook Roscoe's hand.

We were shown to a cozy table nestled near a bay window. Only two other couples were dining on this snowy night. The rosy glow of candles on the tables and the dimmed restaurant lighting reminded me of an old master's oil painting. Roscoe seated us with a flourish and asked

Dr. Hess if he wanted him to chill his favorite Saint Emilion red wine from the Dordogne Valley? Dr. Hess answered with an enthusiastic "yes".

At first I felt awkward and wasn't sure I wanted to say very much. I knew we were both hungry and tired, and I was losing my joie de vivre. There was a stillness between us for a few moments. I thought of the big feather bed at home and wished we had gone directly there from the hospital.

Roscoe appeared with a bottle of wine wrapped in a linen towel. With a flourish he uncorked the bottle and poured a small amount of wine into a wine glass and handed it to Dr. Hess.

"Your opinion, Doctor?"

After a few moments of proper wine testing that involved Dr. Hess twirling the wine in his glass, tilting the glass so that he could admire the "legs" on the wine, and holding the glass before the table's candle light to inspect the magenta color, Dr. Hess said quietly to me, "This color is the same shade of red as the late afternoon sun we saw a few moments ago, don't you think?"

I sat deeper into my chair and began to relax, smiling back at him. Then Dr. Hess brought the wine glass to just below his nose, blew softly above the glass and took a deep sniff. "A subtle aroma, with a hint of cloves, yet almost like fine perfume."

I could hardly wait to hear what he would say next.

He sipped a small amount of wine, held it in his mouth for a few seconds and swished it around in the back of his throat. At that point he smiled broadly, enthusiastically proclaiming, "A mysterious combination of tart and sweet, yet robust and smooth—a fine Dordogne wine."

He turned to Roscoe who stood there in anticipation of Dr. Hess's evaluation. "Excellent, Roscoe; as good as any I've had."

Both Roscoe and the waiter standing nearby seemed to sigh with relief. Roscoe was delighted and signaled to the waiter to place a silver basket of fresh-baked rolls on the table. The waiter poured us each a glass of wine and then placed china salad plates and a silver bowl of rose-shaped butter pats before us and softly walked away, following Roscoe's exit.

Dr. Hess slid his chair a bit closer to the table. His eyes sparkled with golden flecks that mirrored the candle light. "I think you will enjoy the wine tonight," he said.

"Thank you, Dr. Hess," I replied.

He smiled again and winked at me. "Please call me Brad."

I was captivated. (But still could not call him Brad.) We raised our wine glasses and he made a toast, "To us tonight." He touched his glass to mine.

"Yes, to us tonight," I softly echoed his words,

We were famished and began to enthusiastically drink the wine and eat the dinner rolls lavishly coated with butter.

As we ate our dinners, Dr. Hess slightly hesitated and gazed into my eyes.

"I'm glad you are here with me tonight," he softly said as he reached across the table. He took my hand, interlacing his fingers with mine, and kissed my fingertips. With this attention and the lovely glasses of wine and good food I felt my spirits lifting and my tiredness melting away.

We talked about things that we loved: beautiful gardens in Canada and Europe that I had seen, horse races that Dr. Hess had watched.

"I've always wanted to see the Kentucky Derby," I told him.

"Then you shall!" he exclaimed. "I have always wanted to see Paris in the spring."

"Then you shall!" I countered, and we both laughed.

Dr. Hess was suturing this evening just right. He tied together a table full of great food, wonderful wine, warm smiles and good cheer. He kept the conversation light and fun—no hospital stuff or recovery regimens. He was gracious to the restaurant staff and he made me feel happy and secure. For a while after dinner we sat at the table just looking at each other. When we heard a large floor clock strike 7 P.M. we decided it was time to go.

As we got in the car we could see the snowstorm

increasing in intensity again. We had made it to the base of my driveway when Dr. Hess's gallant Escalade got stuck in a snow drift. We slowly pushed the doors open against the heavy snow and started to post-hole our way to my house. The tall ponderosa and white pine trees loomed all around us, swaying lightly to the music of the wind. I hugged my long green Pendleton wool coat around me and tried to wrap the long tartan scarf around my head and shoulders, which proved nearly impossible in the biting wind and relentless snow. Dr. Hess stopped and helped me twist the fringed scarf ends around my head and shoulders. Tears welled in my eyes—it had been a long time since a handsome man had looked after me. To cover up my unexpected tears I laughed instead. He joined in.

I had noticed earlier in the evening that he wore a hip-length, light camel-colored wool coat and didn't seem cold at all. He told me that he hated hats and now he had a mound of snow circling his head and neck. His head looked like a Russian ushanka fur hat with ear flaps. It almost looked like the outline of a proud lion's head and mane covered with snow.

With difficulty, we entered the house across the broad redwood porch. It seemed like we had walked a mile, although we had traveled only a few hundred yards. Dr. Hess held onto my elbow as I clumsily unlocked the large doors. We stumbled through the 8-foot-tall, two-door glassed entryway. I turned to look at Dr. Hess, and we both laughed uproarishly when we saw our reflections in the large floor-to-ceiling mirror on the opposite wall, which I had installed after the recent surgeries so I could study my posture.

As he came through the foyer, Dr. Hess arched his head and neck high into the air and then bent over and began stomping his feet and shaking his body from shoulders to legs. We were both soaked to the skin. Water ran off my coat and boots, pooling around my feet onto the green tiled floor. Strangely enough, though, very little water had pooled beneath Dr. Hess's tall leather boots. He pulled off his jacket and gloves. We kicked off our boots and set them to one side.

"I'll be right back," I said, gathering up all the wet garments and padding down the gold wall-papered hallway. "I'm just going to hang these things up and turn on the big fireplace in the great room to take away the chill."

I walked back quickly and handed Dr. Hess a folded stack of ivory-colored articles consisting of silk pajamas, a cashmere robe, silk slippers and a big Turkish towel. I always keep spare silk lounging pajamas and slippers for my guests and myself. I could see he was impressed. I explained that my sons often visited me so I have learned to be prepared, hence the men's pajamas, robe and slippers.

"We have sudden, unexpected harsh weather up here," I lamely added. "They have been stuck here over night on a few occasions." This was such an understatement that we both laughed again.

"Sure, sure," he said smiling, "and not any other men friends, I suppose?"

I glowed beet-red in embarrassment. At my side, the object of my intense desire, an older and wiser Dr. Hess was with me in my home tonight. I had dreamed of this moment. It was too good to be true. I hoped I would not ruin this. How will I respond if—when—he slips into my bed? I have been known to be rather cold in bed; my late husband often told me so. It had been a long time since I shared my bed with anyone except a cat.

"A washing machine and dryer are near the guest bedroom where you can put your things tonight. I have a washer and dryer near my bedroom at the other side of the house and I'll do the same."

I sounded ridiculous and hoped I would quit talking like this. "Let's shed the rest of the wet stuff and meet in the library at the other end of the hall."

His reflection in the mirror appeared majestic, regal. I had forgotten that he was not a tall man, not much taller than my 5-foot, 8-inch frame, but he seemed taller. He had a broad neck and muscular chest, legs and arms. He reached down to the tip of his toes, then stretched up toward the ceiling with his fingertips and turned toward me with a smile. I felt a surge of warmth radiating from my hips to the roots of my hair. I had never been so enamored.

Wind and snow howled across the large windows of the library. We sipped brandy in bubble-shaped, rainbow-colored glass brandy snifters while sitting together on a cognac-colored leather couch. Self-consciously I tucked a small lemon silk pillow between my knees to keep from trying to cross my legs. Crossing your legs is a no-no after hip replacement and I had a hard time remembering that. I thought Dr. Hess would correct me and I didn't want to be his patient now. I wanted to be his equal, his partner; wanted much, much more. I wanted the rosy glow feeling I felt at dinner—the way he held my chair out as I sat down, the way he tilted my chin and brushed his lips to my ear … the way he looked at me across the table and stroked and held my hand … the way he smiled and winked at me.

We had the smaller gas fireplace in the library turned up against the bitter cold. Cranberry, burnt orange and yellow flames dazzled our eyes and made shadows on the opposite wall. My three cats were curled up cozily in the russet and gold velvet chairs grouped around the fireplace. They were not afraid of Dr. Hess at all. This was a surprise because whenever a new person came to visit, my big male cat Jo-Jo usually runs under one of the ruffle-skirted beds. My two old girl-kitties, Lotsie-Lou and T-Mu, mysteriously disappear to places unknown. I had also noticed that they uncharacteristically met us at the front door. Dr. Hess—now I felt I could call him Brad—had met each one and stroked their backs from head to tail, which endeared him to me even more.

Brad kicked off his slippers and was toasting his feet before the fire, spreading his toes to dry. I was struck by the fine golden hair on his ankles and toes. In fact, while eating dinner, I had noticed the same fine golden hair on the backs of his hands and fingers.

In spite of my resolve, I kept seeing visions of the first time I was with him at the hospital. I shook my head at recalling those hallucinations. I thought he had turned into a cougar, saved my life and made love to me in the hospital bed. Then as I rode high on his broad back, he took me to Estes Park and circled my home and his lion's den, which was only a mountain away. I dismissed those thoughts later as being a side effect of opium-based painkillers. Was that when I started having trouble discerning reality, or maybe that was when I slipped into another universe? Wouldn't Brad be surprised if he knew my thoughts?

We talked about many things. Brad told me the reason he became an orthopedic surgeon was because his mother suffered for years with rheumatoid arthritis and his sister died from a crushed pelvis after a tragic car accident. He told me he had grown up poor and was determined to make a good living and help people at the same time. I told him that I had a very unhappy marriage (something I rarely admitted). I also had grown up poor and was determined to be the first person in my family to get a college education; determined that my two sons receive good educations. He asked how my writing was progressing. (I knew I had told him I wanted to be a writer, but I wasn't sure that I had told him about this in my dream or in reality.) He rotated his shoulders backward against the large leather cushions and smiled contentedly. The topic of our conversations came back to the two of us as a couple—the changes that were happening to each of us.

Brad spoke softly, "I can feel it inside me. I am freer. I see you blossoming. Each time we are together time stops, yet speeds up."

I looked away, letting this sink in.

"Do you remember when I told you we were soul mates?" Brad's question startled me as I thought that was my memory alone: another hallucination that wasn't. "I sensed that the moment I met you."

My mystical reverie was broken when Brad received a phone call on his iPhone, which he had placed in his bathrobe pocket after he shed his wet clothes. (Of course, being a doctor, he kept his phone near him.) I remember each detail in slow motion. He stood up and told me it was an important call from the Estes Park hospital. He stretched again and gracefully walked barefooted to the entryway to take the call. He was on the phone for a long time. I could hear him pacing back and forth.

I was hypnotized by the hearth's multi-colored flames and went back to my earlier reverie: I continued to update my dreams. I thought how easily we had come back together after that last time in the hospital, our dinner tonight, his reflection in my mirror. He was here. He was really here. I shivered with happiness and anticipation of the rest of my night with him.

I heard Brad say rather loudly, "No, no, not that way. If my assistant Davis is handy I will walk him through the steps."

I thought, *Is Brad's assistant Davis also up here in Estes Park? Davis must be staying at the hospital on this bitter cold night.*

He kept talking on the phone, and I continued to think back, *I will go crazy if I don't separate my dreams from reality. I may have coped well physically with my surgeries, but I have not coped well mentally. Look how I still dwell on them.* The hip revision surgery was harder than the knee replacement and much harder than the first hip replacement. I don't remember my son and grandsons bringing me home after hip surgery in June. I lost a whole day and even now cannot reconstruct the drive from the hospital through Denver, Boulder and the Rocky Mountain foothills, up the canyon to my mountain home. *Why can't I let it all go? Maybe my brain has been permanently altered.*

Eventually, Brad came back into the library, stood in front of the fireplace and faced me.

"Sorry that took so long," he said. "We are setting up a clinic at the Estes Park hospital tomorrow to train therapists in the new treatments for joint replacement patients. I am having difficulty getting through to some of the mountain nursing staff and have asked Davis to take charge tomorrow. He has a down-to-earth approach with everyone. By the way, they told me the storm is intensifying and wondered if we would want to come back to the hospital. The basement there is totally secure with emergency food, heat and lighting, in case we have a blackout and are buried in snow."

"What did you tell them?" I asked.

"I said you have a wonderful, well-equipped mountain house built to withstand harsh weather and that we will do fine. I didn't tell them that my car is buried in tons of snow at the foot of your driveway." His chuckle came from somewhere deep within his chest. I shifted positions on the couch and looked up to face him directly.

We both became still. He looked at me like he was

making a diagnosis. Then he very slowly and quietly walked toward me, toeing in slightly. He stood massive over me and looked down at me with his gold-flecked, deep-set eyes. The pupils of his eyes were large, dark and oval-shaped. He took off his robe and pajama top and crouched beside me. Hardly making a sound he reached over and gently turned my face to his. He traced the flickering outline of flames from the fireplace on my face, down my neck and into the v-necked opening of my robe as he eased me out of my robe and pajama top. The silk pillow slid from between my legs onto the floor. He gently kissed me with his large and soft lips. I could feel the soft stubble of chin whiskers, the faint scent of expensive aftershave—musky, mysterious, moist.

He parted my lips with his tongue and kissed me deeply, taking my breath away. I passionately kissed him back and stroked his broad shoulders and back. He shifted his position. Lying on his left side he pulled me sideways, facing me outward toward the fireplace. He tucked me into his broad chest and strong legs. We fit perfectly within the long contours of the soft leather couch. He stroked my breasts and pulled down my pajama bottoms. He stroked the tender mound between my legs, fingering inside me.

He murmured, "I feel you." An electric current shot through me. I saw the flickering of the fireplace and heard a purring sound. I had trouble focusing my eyes. Then my ears were buzzing. I saw stars. I was quivering. He turned me onto my stomach and placed the silk pillow under my hips, lifting me upward toward him. I felt a large tail go between my legs. He hesitated a moment and mounted me from behind. He entered me carefully, expertly. I heard panting from both of us and saw the shadows of our bodies reflected on the opposite wall: up and down, back and forth, soft and slow, fast and hard. My body responded and yielded completely. This rhythm went on and on. A simultaneous release of pressure, then a wet surge up, up, up … a great hot rippling that cycled almost painfully— pulsing, gripping, tearing, spreading from my loins to my breasts. My entire body convulsed. Oh, the thrill of it! My body and brain were on fire.

I lifted my head and saw a large cougar's head reflected on the wall, hair falling down his neck and over his forehead. He lifted himself above me, rested on his elbows, took a deep breath, threw back his head and roared gustfully. I was fearful and ecstatic, satiated and terrified. I didn't want the sensations to stop or to continue: I couldn't stand it anymore; but I couldn't stand this to stop. I was disintegrating, dissolving beneath him.

Some time passed before we could physically separate. Finally we rested together, his hands overlapping my breasts.

Native Americans observed fully mature male cougars coupling with their mates. He courts her with strokes, sniffing and nuzzles. He tumbles her down to lie by his side and wraps his heavy tail between her legs. When he and his partner are sufficiently aroused as evidenced by their heavy digging, breathing and panting, he positions her beneath him and mounts her from behind. The coupling has periods of gentle and violent movements with no rest periods in between. The act can take several minutes. It also takes a while for the pair to decouple: his swelling is often twice normal size. The female feels depleted and must rest afterward to regain her strength. The male cougar leaves her shortly afterward wandering off to recover by himself.

I was exhausted. I stretched out on my back on the couch, and Brad placed the lemon yellow silk pillow under my head and covered me with the couch's scarlet-green-yellow tartan afghan. He knelt beside me for a few moments and stroked my hair back from my eyes, kissing me softly. Before I fell asleep I heard him get up and pad softly away into the guest bedroom.

Three hours later, he came back into the library fully dressed. He talked animatedly, and I was trying to follow what he was saying, but I was still groggy with sleep.

"Hear that?" he asked.

I became aware of the sound of large tree branches cracking and shearing off from the over-loaded, snow-covered trees. They were crashing to the ground, piercing the earth like javelins—*zing, bang, crash.* Brad told me to get fully dressed in warm clothes and boots and help him gather blankets, food and water. I came back into the kitchen dressed in my warmest clothes and boots. Brad was busy gathering food supplies. He had my three cats in cat carriers placed on the kitchen counter.

I remember thinking, *This man is amazing to think of the cats at a time like this.* Then we heard it—an ear-shattering crack, almost an animal moan, like a ship going down at sea, and an enormous crash.

"My God!" I yelled. "A big tree just fell into my house! The roof is exploding!"

The steep, peaked, log framed roof above us was being torn apart. Big logs from the ceiling crashed behind us, blocking the kitchen from the rest of the house. Portions of the tree trunk, enormous branches, pine needles and cones fell all around us, pinning us into a tight circle. Enormous mounds of snow fell in and buried us. Brad and I were yelling at each other, as the cats shrieked and banged against their carriers out of the sheer fright of the scene.

In what was to become known as the biggest blizzard

to hit Estes Park in 200 years, it snowed in everyone for three days. Fifty-one people were killed in the ravaging storm—some in their homes and other buildings, some on the roads, some caught outside. Even though my home was mountain-built with extra thick walls and reinforced roofs, we were hit hard. The forest around us with its uprooted and falling-apart, snow-laden trees endangered us. As I heard the trees breaking apart, thoughts raced through my mind. Even if we could leave the house, we probably could not make it down the driveway. If we could make it down the driveway, we could never dig out Brad's car. If we could dig out Brad's car, large trees had probably crushed it. Even if that had not happened, we couldn't make it out. The roads would be impassable.

We had nowhere to hide, nowhere to go—or so I thought.

I woke up in a cave bundled in blankets. My cougar was gathering small branches and rolling them into bundles and filling the entrance. I was lying on a large elk skin with my three cats huddled next to me. Brad began to tell me what had been happening.

"After the roof caved in I carried you and your cats into my den."

I interrupted, "How did you do that?"

"On my back," he said. "I flew through the tremendous, debris-filled winter storm. This is one of the worst storms I can remember."

"How far away from my home is this den?" I almost hesitated to ask.

"Do you remember us flying over your house and my den when you were in the hospital after your knee replacement?"

I looked perplexed then remembered—the den was a mountain away just southwest of my house, located in very rocky steep terrain.

Native Americans say the male cougar will take a special partner to explore the territory he patrols and show her his den. If he takes her to his den, he means to keep her as a mate with him for life. But he rarely takes any female cougar to his den.

The wind whipped around our shelter, carrying his unbuttoned coat and tawny-colored hair upward and around him. Brad breathed rapidly. He raced in and outside the den gathering branches and breaking them apart, wrapping them in bundles. I moved closer to the entrance.

"Tell me more," I shouted over the roar of the storm.

Well," he began, "large ponderosa branches too heavy to hold the snow started shearing off and plummeting to the ground all around and on top of your house. I'm sorry to tell you that your biggest ponderosa, Raggedy Ann, was pulled up by the roots and crashed on the steepest part of the roof, over the great room and kitchen areas. I've dragged some of the smaller branches here to secure the opening of our hiding place."

I nodded my head, which felt disconnected from the rest of my body. "Yes, I remember."

Brad continued, "One of the largest branches pierced through the roof where we were standing and knocked you unconscious. So far, I have made half a dozen trips from your house to my lair, bringing in supplies. I have also alerted Davis as to our whereabouts. I told him if he does not see us by Sunday dusk to come get us."

"What day? What time is this?" I asked.

"It's Saturday afternoon about 3 P.M. It will be getting dark outside soon and the cave will be pitch-black. I must get the entrance to my lair secure to keep out the cold, wind and drifting snow and keep out other wild animals that may have been dislodged from their dens in the storm."

He emphasized the last few words, and I wondered about this. I could not imagine any animals being out in a storm like this. I believed they would stay in their dens even if they were broken apart. Brad's lair was discretely hidden behind an oblique opening under large rock outcroppings. When we flew over it a year ago, I had difficulty seeing the entrance from above. Brad had passed over the cave again carefully flying lower and from a sharp northeast angle to make sure I saw the cave's opening. Nevertheless, I wasn't sure I had seen it. This cave, a tunnel actually (perhaps a gold mine exploration tunnel a century ago), was 8 feet tall and dozens of feet long. It narrowed as it progressed into the rock outcropping above. A wide rock ledge appeared to be at the cave's entrance and then a near vertical slope down the mountain, which in summertime is covered by small trees, sage, sumac and cinquefoil bushes. Brad told me he wanted to obscure this ledge with branches, as well as the entrance. From where I sat, the walls consisted of lichen-covered granite that appeared to remain moist yearlong from summer snows, spring runoff and heavy winter snowmelt as indicated by the moss growing in the cracks. What I had immediately noticed when I was aware of my surroundings was the wet, musky, peat moss and sage smell of the cave.

Brad spoke rapidly, motioning next to the wall. "Perhaps you can open the large bag and take out the knife and food. We haven't eaten since Friday evening, so we need something to eat. We had better make sandwiches before it gets dark."

I clumsily opened the bag and took out a very large,

long-handled bread knife. I must have had this in my kitchen but had forgotten about it.

"We have a good shaft of light coming through the entrance right now," Brad continued, "but soon I'll block off much of that with branches and then nighttime will fall. I keep the den somewhat supplied with animal skins, blankets and such, but I do not keep much food or water."

"How long can we stay here?" I asked.

"I hope we have enough food to last us through the weekend. The cats can eat cut-up lunch meat. We can eat snow for water. We'll have to wrap ourselves and the cat carriers with elk hides. It will get cold tonight. By the way, I couldn't find a flashlight, lantern or candles at your home."

"Those were on my list to buy," I replied. "Did you bring any utensils or plates?" I didn't want to place our sandwiches on dirty blankets to eat.

"The only utensil we have is the large kitchen knife, which we will have to use for everything: cutting branches, any digging that we must do to bury our wastes as well as for food preparation."

I was not surprised to hear him say all of this. That is the way his brilliant mind worked: rapid fire, all-encompassing thoughts about our situation, coming up with quick plans and solutions.

We were both silent. Then I asked almost timidly, "Is my home ruined?"

Brad reflected, "Not all of it—just the west side. It can be rebuilt. It is a shame that the mighty ponderosa pine and white pine trees were uprooted."

"The greatest loss to me is Raggedy Ann," I added sadly.

Trying to beat the waning light, I worked on making sandwiches, cutting the cheese and meat to fill the slices of bread that I had spread out on a blanket before me. Brad was in the entryway dragging in more branches.

Suddenly the room darkened and everything went quiet. I heard strange pawing, scraping and guttural sounds from the entrance to the cave. As I looked up, Brad was on all fours, his back to me facing a large black bear, also on all fours. They pawed at each other and then wrestled, swiping and raking each other's heads, necks and shoulders. Brad yelled at me to go to the back of the cave. My cats scattered and ran every which way. I was paralyzed with fear and crouched on my knees with the big bread knife in my hand.

Brad's form was no longer that of a man. He was a large male cougar fiercely battling one of the biggest bears I have ever seen, as tall as the cave entrance and three times the cougar's size. Lightning fast, the bear backed Brad into the den, toward me. The shuffling sounds and loud growls were deafening. The male cougar swiped the bear with knife-sharp claws—shrieking, panting and hissing—sounds reverberating off the cave's walls. The bear growled and bellowed a deeper sound, swiping at the cougar's head, trying to tear out his eyes and scrape off his ears. His paws were enormous—at least 5 inches wide—with black talon claws half as long. He smelled wild, mean and reeked of animal feces and urine.

I watched them fight, the back legs of each animal planted firmly on the cave's floor, talons dug into the loose earth. The cougar's leg muscles bulged, tendons extended, looking like writhing snakes. The bear's legs were huge and post-like, its shaggy black fur quivering under his bulk and the effort of the fight. By surprising strength, the cougar backed the bear out of the cave entrance.

"He's trying to move the bear out of his lair, trying to protect us!" I gasped to myself out of sheer panic, the adrenaline coursing through my veins

With all of his might, Brad stood up with the bear, wrapping their arms around each other. Sharp claws tore and gouged each other's backs and arms. Drooling saliva ran down their chins and blood dripped down their sides, arms and legs. They lumbered farther out of the cave's entrance onto the rock shelf. In the dim light I saw the bear swipe at the cougar's chest and arms. Brad's right arm dangled down his side. Was it dislocated or nearly torn away? How would he ever operate again?

Grabbing the large bread knife firmly in my hands, I swung into action and ran into the maelstrom of animal fury, positioning myself between the heaving bodies when they momentarily broke apart. I held the knife in both hands stabbing into the bear's neck. I first missed as the blade slid off the slick fur and then, bringing it down again, it met the mark, plunging deep into the bear's neck and jugular vein. Blood squirted out, covering all three of us. I was temporarily blinded from the wild winds blowing the blood at every angle. I fully expected to be killed in the next instant and tried to root myself more firmly to the rock shelf. Instead, I heard a series of shudders and a rush of hot air as if being expelled from a hot-air balloon. An enormous furry form plummeted to the ground, shaking the earth around us.

We slumped to the rocky entrance of the cougar's lair. Twig bundles had blown away and the rock ledge was slick and covered with blood running down the snowy white mountain slope turning the steep sides magenta and pink.

The bear was dead; the cougar near death. "God help us!" I cried out hysterically. Sobbing and wiping at my eyes, I collapsed on the cold rock shelf.

It took me over the next two hours to gather my strength and drag the cougar into the cave. His heart was still beating and his breaths came in rapid bursts. After binding his nearly severed arm tightly to his side, I wrapped him in two large elk skin rugs and used the third elk skin to wrap around my cats and me. We all fell into a heap. I cried in choking sobs, then hiccups and soon fell asleep, too exhausted to endure any more.

> *Native Americans believed if a male cougar enters your life he does so to teach you about your own power. You are at a crossroads in your life and must choose what direction you will follow. The male cougar will stay close to your side for the rest of his life if you are brave enough and make the right choice. The male cougar is always searching and chooses a mate who can teach him something new.*

I woke up in total blackness. Brad was awake and spoke in his usual analytical surgeon style. He seemed to be hallucinating.

"I was thinking about this when I was dreaming and how brains become altered," he said. "What was happening to us? Brain scan researchers are now saying that when a person is in love both the right and left hemispheres of the brain are highly activated. They have also noted that when you learn to play a musical instrument the corpus callosum, the part of the brain that mediates contact between the left and right hemispheres, grows thicker with hours of practicing, studying and listening to music. The thicker fibers provide more pathways for insightful and creative communication which greatly enriches the music."

We both dozed again.

He startled me when he asked, "You are learning to play the flute aren't you?"

I just gazed at him.

"I don't think you know I play the clarinet. We should play together sometime."

I cradled his shaggy, bloody head in my arms and wrapped the elk blanket tightly around his arms and shoulders. I believed he was dying.

"I'd love to play with you sometime," I consoled him.

After several hours we were both awake again. Brad whispered. "Haven't you noticed that each time we are together our conversations deepen and become richer?"

I suspected he had lost a lot of blood and did not know what he was saying.

He continued, "What I was trying to tell you earlier: we know our conversational channels grow thicker. In simplistic terms the left side deals with logic—the Greeks called this Logos. The right side deals with emotion and intuition—the Greeks called this Eros. Did you know that physical and emotional well-being needs both music and love? Both Logos and Eros enrich the brain by integrating the two. Our union is improving our imagination, emotional sensitivity, coordination and dexterity. Together we are formidable like a great symphony, greater than all of the instruments."

Brad was clearly hallucinating. I always wanted a brilliant man. Even in his dying state, he was brilliant. I felt that all of us in this cave were dying. It was so cold in here, and I was so hungry. He dozed off again.

He jarred me when he spoke. I thought he was unconscious. "You were very brave tonight. You were very loving and very brave."

I wrapped myself up tightly, curled close to him and listened to his deep breaths, knowing full well it would stop soon. It would become more labored, then swift and shallow, then loud and soft.

I saw a flash through the cave's entrance. Was it lightning? Was sunlight filtering in? I heard the transformer on the mountain above my home come back to life. *Zing-Buzz-Humm ...* Power was being restored. What day was it? Sunday? Monday? Suddenly I saw a man standing in the entrance of the cave—legs apart, getting his bearing and surveying the scene. He shone a large flashlight in and around the cave. Then he saw us. It was Davis.

"Davis is here!" I caressed Brad. "Davis is here and he will save all of us."

Davis turned his head and I saw a magnificent profile—a great young cougar inside the man—the same brilliant, proud and capable persona that I had seen so many times in my own cougar.

Afterword

What I wanted to tell Brad that night in the cougar den but probably never will was that despite our age difference of 17 years, we formed a mysterious bond. People talk about chemistry uniting a couple; I think it is electricity. A warm golden aura surrounds us when we are together. Another way I think about our attraction is that we fit together like the two halves of a Chinese ying-yang Tao symbol. I imagine that I am the white part of the Tao symbol; Brad is the black part.

When I was a college student I once saw a couple dancing at a dance club one afternoon. Their bodies blended into each other so that their bodies' boundaries seemed indistinguishable. She was smaller than he was and her body tucked quite perfectly into the curves of his long, strong torso and legs. Her head rested under his chin, resembling the Tao symbol.

Just like the couple on the dance floor, Brad and I fit together like two key pieces of a jigsaw puzzle. Together we represent unity, polarity, holism and magic. Our two halves revolve about each other in perfect balance yet are constantly interacting, never in an absolute state, always changing.

> *Native Americans have observed the female cougar in a life-long relationship with her mate. She reinforces the attentiveness of the male cougar by preserving her feminine mystique. She does not fully reveal her innermost thoughts or intentions. She shows her commitment in other ways—loving, generosity, bravery and intelligence.*

Davis saved Brad, me and my cats. Brad quit his medical practice in Denver after he lost the use of his right arm. He kept his apartment in Denver and moved into my home in Estes Park. We married a few months later. We rebuilt my home, which we restored and enlarged. He has become a much sought after international orthopedic consultant. Davis has taken over Brad's former medical practice and they keep in close touch.

Brad's cougar died in the fight with the black bear.

Native Americans believed that the Cougar God bestows honors to the male cougar after death. The levels of honor are first in defending his territory, second in defending his den and the greatest honor of all is defending and preserving the life of his partner.

I have no doubt that I am living in one universe. I no longer have the hallucinations I had in the past. What happened was meant to happen. Brad and I have been happily together ten years. I'm going for twenty more: I will be a hundred years old then. With Brad, I just might make it.

About the Author

VIOLET LEE HUNT is a Colorado native, born and raised in Boulder. A fan of the short story writing genre and prolific author of numerous short story collections, Ms. Hunt began her writing career as a budding journalist in high school and college, working as an editor and reporter for the school newspapers. During her college years, her interests moved in a different direction.

After receiving degrees in chemistry and computer science from the University of Colorado she refocused her creative writing abilities toward technical writing while pursuing a successful career as a computer engineer and corporate executive in the computer science field. In addition she has been a science and math teacher, lecturer and business owner. She founded her own business processing company Vi Hunt, Inc. (2000–2006) in Boulder, Colorado.

An author of two previously published books on computer science, Ms. Hunt has written and conducted numerous workshops on software engineering. In addition she authored a monthly column on information engineering for IBM for two years.

Since leaving the computer engineering industry, Ms. Hunt has returned to her early roots and today actively commits her time and energies to her two biggest passions—creative writing and travel to exotic destinations.

She is a prolific writer of short stories and books for the senior women market. Her books are filled with spark and excitement, with many of her stories centered around the love lives of couples, unrequited love, as well as love gone sour. The characters in her stories are tinged with vacillating elements of sadness and glory, full of confidence, yet vulnerable to the varied passions that love's wind blows.

Including *Injured Cougar,* she is the author of three other published books: two short story collections—*Lavender Muse: Three Short Stories About Women Who Find True Friends in Former Strangers* and *Patterns of Deceit: Four Couples' Stories of Love Lost,* and the nonfiction story *Cottage in the Clouds.*

She has two forthcoming nonfiction books being published in 2012: *Notes from the Past: A Rocky Mountain Adventure* and *Growing Up on Concord.*

A mother, grandmother, and animal lover, Ms. Hunt lives in Estes Park, Colorado, with her two cats.